First published in Great Britain in 1978 by Andersen Press Ltd., 20 Vauxhall Bridge Road,
London SW1V 2SA. Published in Australia by Random House Australia Pty. Ltd.,
20 Alfred Street, Milsons Point, Sydney NSW 2061. All rights reserved.
Colour separated by Photolitho AG Offsetreproduktionen, Gossau, Zürich, Switzerland.
Printed and bound in Italy by Grafiche AZ, Verona. ISBN 0-905478-37-1

2 3 4 5 6 7 8 9

Grandma was a nice, scatty old lady, who was clever with her sewing machine. As shop prices were so high, she made lots of clothes for the little girl, most of them in her favourite colour, red.

One day, she made a lovely cape, with a hood on it.

A RED one!

The little girl wore her new cape whenever she went out on her bike.
The woodcutter sometimes puffed along behind her, warning her of the rabbit holes, and hidden tree roots. All the small animals stayed well out of her way.
"Don't play in the traffic!" they told their children.
Soon the little girl became known as Little Red Riding Hood.

One fine afternoon in August, the little girl's mum packed some of Grandma's favourite things in a bag: some homemade tarts and pickles, a bottle of stout, and the paper with the weekend television programmes in it.

Little Red Riding Hood set off on her weekly visit to Grandma's house. Her parents walked down to the bottom of the field with her.

"Hurry straight to Grandma's," they called, waving goodbye. "Don't play about on the way, and don't lose yourself in daydreams!"

The little girl skipped along, whistling silly tunes.
Suddenly she saw a *huge* dog, fast asleep under a tree.
The dog was really a WOLF, although Red Riding Hood didn't
know that. Plucking a piece of grass, she tickled the wolf on the
nose. He opened one beady eye.

The wolf was hungry, and he *had* thought of eating the little girl, but it then occurred to him that if he was clever he could eat the grandmother too.

"No need to rush, on a warm day like this," said the wolf, in an oily voice. "Why not stay a while, enjoy the flowers, and the fine sun?"

The sun *was* warm, and the wolf's words were *very* sensible, so Red Riding Hood sat down on a log, and began to make a daisy chain.

When her back was turned, the wolf sneaked away. His plan was to go to Grandma's house, and eat her for dinner, then when Red Riding Hood arrived, he'd have her for pudding.

The wolf rang Grandma's doorbell.
Grandma had just settled down to watch the news.
"Who's there?" she muttered, not happy at having to
get up again.

Squeezing his nose through the letterbox, the wolf used his squeakiest voice, "'Tis I, Little Red Riding Hood!" Grandma's face lit up.
"Come in, dear!" she cried, throwing open the door.

The wolf pounced through the open door, and swallowed Grandma in one gulp, for she was a very little old lady.

Hiccupping gently, the wolf put the second part of his plan into action. He trotted upstairs to the bedroom, put on Grandma's biggest night things, and sprang into bed to wait for Red Riding Hood.

He felt very silly dressed up like that, but he *had* to look like an old lady. Catching sight of himself in the mirror, the wolf didn't think he looked much like Grandma, so he leapt out of bed in a flurry of pink flannel, and switched off the light.

Dusk was gathering as Red Riding Hood knocked at Grandma's door.

"Come in, dearie," called the wolf. "I'm upstairs, lying down!" He tried to sound like Grandma now.

Red Riding Hood crept into the darkened bedroom, and jumped onto the bed.

Although the wolf hid as much of himself as possible, the little girl couldn't help noticing . . .

"OH GRANDMA, WHAT BIG EARS YOU'VE GOT!" she said.

"All the better to HEAR you with, my dear!" mumbled the wolf.

Little Red Riding Hood looked more closely at the shape in the bed.
"AND WHAT BIG EYES YOU'VE GOT!" she said.
The wolf was rather proud of his eyes.
"All the better to SEE you with!" he said, eyelashes a-flutter.

When Red Riding Hood touched a huge, hairy paw, she felt that things were just not right.

"And Grandma," she said, "WHAT BIG HANDS YOU'VE GOT!"

"All the better to HUG you with!" rumbled the wolf.

He was beginning to ease himself out of the bed, and the faint light flashed on his teeth.

"A- A- A- ND WHAT BIG TEETH YOU'VE GOT!" stammered the little girl.

"ALL THE BETTER TO EAT YOU WITH!" howled the wolf, and with a swirl of bed clothes and pink nightie, he snatched the little girl, and swallowed her in one gulp.
Then he gobbled the homemade tarts, and drank the brown ale.

Feeling full, and very pleased with himself, the wolf staggered downstairs, and collapsed on the floor, in dreamy, food-filled sleep.

Meanwhile, the woodcutter, worried by his daughter's long absence, was searching the woods for her.
He lit his way with the torch he got for Christmas, and he carried his big axe in case he met anything nasty.

Peeping through Grandma's open door, the woodcutter spied the wolf, snoring gently on the floor. He also saw the wolf's *huge* tummy. Realising what had happened, the woodcutter leapt forward, bringing his axe down with a stunning blow on the wolf's head. Grabbing the unlucky animal by the feet, the woodcutter bounced him up and down until both Red Riding Hood and Grandma tumbled out of the wolf's mouth.

They sat blinking on the floor, angry and sticky, but otherwise unhurt.

When the wolf woke up, he RAN and RAN and RAN.
Grandma and Red Riding Hood pelted him
with everything they could lay their
hands on, to speed him on his
way. Even the small
animals joined in,
for wolves are no
friends of theirs.

The woodcutter took Red Riding Hood and Grandma home with him, and Mother made a super supper for everyone.
The wolf moved to another district and gave up trying to eat people. He tried to grow vegetables instead, although he wasn't much good at that, either.